JACK JOUETT'S RIDE

WRITTEN AND ILLUSTRATED BY

GAIL E. HALEY

The Viking Press   New York

First published in 1973 by The Viking Press, Inc., 625 Madison Avenue, New York, N.Y. 10022
Published simultaneously in Canada by The Macmillan Company of Canada Limited
Library of Congress catalog card number: 73–5137
Printed in U.S.A.
Pic Bk
SBN 670–40466–7
1 2 3 4 5 77 76 75 74 73

This book is dedicated to the memory of Velma V. Varner

Acknowledgments: The author wishes to thank
Arnold, Marguerite, and Geoffrey;
Lady Walton for suggesting that this book be written;
Douglas Tanner, Virginius Dabney, and the many individuals
and organizations who aided in the research,
including the state and county historical societies
of Virginia and Kentucky, representatives of
federal, state, and local committees of the American
Revolution Bicentennial, and archivists at
Williamsburg, Monticello, the University of Virginia,
the Library of Congress, and the British Museum,
among others.

Jack Jouett was sitting in the moonlight
outside Cuckoo Tavern when he heard the clink
and clatter of riding cavalry.
But what soldiers could be riding,
in the still and hush of evening? Everyone
thought the British were many miles away.

He crept softly to the roadside. What he saw there froze his blood. It was Tarleton, "Bloody Tarleton," King George's hunting leopard, and his troop of Green Dragoons, riding hard toward Charlottesville. Jack knew at once whom they meant to capture there.

Thomas Jefferson, Patrick Henry, and other revolutionaries slept in their beds at the end of that road. The colonists needed these men in their fight to become free.

Jack saddled and bridled his bay mare Sallie. There was no one else to carry the alarm.

It was forty miles from Cuckoo to the
town of Charlottesville, and Tarleton's men
were riding on the only road. Jack
Jouett rode across meadows, through thickets,
woods, and mire, with only owls to
cheer him on and the moon to light his way.

Branches tore his skin and
clothing, but he hardly noticed.
He was afraid the British
would arrive before he did.

Luck was with Jack Jouett.
The troops did not know that he'd seen them
and was racing through the night.

So they stopped three times along the way:
first to rest their horses,
then to burn an American wagon train
they had captured on the road.

They stopped the third time at Castle Hill, where two legislators slept. Tarleton's men dragged them from their beds and arrested them in their nightshirts.

Then they say that Tarleton laughed and shouted, "On to Charlottesville, Dragoons; bigger game is yet ahead!"

But Jack Jouett's brave horse Sallie never stopped the whole night through. When they reached the ford at Milton, he knew that he had won.

"Wake up, ferryman; carry us across! I must warn the governor that the British ride this way."

Up at Monticello breakfast fires
were being lighted as the ragged, weary
rider pounded on the door.
The governor listened gravely to
Jack's breathless warning:

"You must ride away at once! Tarleton's men
are riding here to capture you!"

But Thomas Jefferson would not leave
until he had hidden all the state papers
that the British hoped to find.

Jack rode on to his father's inn, the Swan,
where other assemblymen were staying.

The people of Charlottesville gathered to hear
his news: "Hide the women and children;
bar your doors and stay inside.
The British are coming to capture our town."

A handful of militia
rushed to hold them at the river.

Patrick Henry and the others got up from their breakfast and rode across the mountain to meet again another day.

But General Stevens, who had been wounded, was too weak to ride so far. The Jouetts disguised him in a ragged cloak and helped him mount a nag, while Jack put on a fresh uniform and borrowed his father's swiftest horse.

When Tarleton saw that bright red coat
with epaulets and braid, he
thought Jack was an officer of high rank.
"Go after him, men," he shouted.

So Jack Jouett led the British a long and merry
chase while General Stevens slipped away.

Jack Jouett spurred his horse to the top
of a high hill, leaving Tarleton
and his winded troops below. Then he turned,
waved his hat, and cried:

"When men need to be free from tyrants,
they will always find a way."

And these words are as true today as they
were long ago.

EPILOGUE

In recognition of his ride the General Assembly of the State of Virginia voted on June 15, 1781, that "an elegant sword and a pair of pistols" be awarded to Jack Jouett by the grateful government. After the end of the hostilities Jack moved to Kentucky. There he married his childhood sweetheart, Sallie Robards, and fathered twelve children. His son, Matthew Harris Jouett, became one of America's foremost portrait painters. A grandson of Jack Jouett's stood by Admiral Farragut's side at the battle of Mobile Bay.

Jack Jouett was close to President Andrew Jackson, and he remained the personal friend of many of the leaders of the new nation. He helped Kentucky achieve statehood, served four terms in the state legislature, and prospered as a planter and horse breeder. Sallie, the bay mare that carried Jack Jouett on his ride, became the ancestor of a long line of thoroughbreds, some of which still graze in Kentucky's blue grass meadows.